Armadillo on a pillow

Russell Punter

Illustrated by David Semple

Armadillo feels sleepy.
But his pillow's too small.

TING-a-LING! rings a bell.
Stars twinkle and swish.

"A soft, silky pillow would
fit the bill, please."

PING! The sheets billow.
"You can choose one of these."

Armadillo is thrilled.

"What a shame my bed's old.

Will you give me a new one
of silver and gold?"

"Very well," says the fairy.

Armadillo wants more...

"Now I need a grand mansion
with bedrooms galore!"

"Plus a marshmallow mountain!
And what next? I know!

A hot chocolate fountain
that flows down just so!"

A little while later...

"Oh, what have I done?
I've been far too greedy.

Being rich is no fun."

"I feel so ashamed."
He hangs down his head.

"How I wish I was back
in my dear little bed."

Armadillo wakes up
and turns on the light.

"It was all just a dream,"
he sighs with delight.

But his pillow is bigger!
"Now how can that be?"

About phonics

Phonics is a method of teaching reading which is used extensively in today's schools. At its heart is an emphasis on identifying the *sounds* of letters, or combinations of letters, that are then put together to make words. These sounds are known as phonemes.

Starting to read
Learning to read is an important milestone for any child. The process can begin well before children start to learn letters and put them together to read words. The sooner children can discover books and enjoy stories and language, the better they will be prepared for reading themselves, first with the help of an adult and then independently.

You can find out more about phonics on the Usborne Very First Reading website, **www.usborne.com/veryfirstreading** (US readers go to **www.veryfirstreading.com**). Click on the **Parents** tab at the top of the page, then scroll down and click on **About synthetic phonics**.

Phonemic awareness

An important early stage in pre-reading and early reading is developing phonemic awareness: that is, listening out for the sounds within words. Rhymes, rhyming stories and alliteration are excellent ways of encouraging phonemic awareness.

In this story, your child will soon identify the *o* sound, as in **armadillo** and **marshmallow**. Look out, too, for rhymes such as **pillow** – **billow** and **old** – **gold**.

Hearing your child read

If your child is reading a story to you, don't rush to correct mistakes, but be ready to prompt or guide if he or she is struggling. Above all, do give plenty of praise and encouragement.

Edited by Jenny Tyler and Lesley Sims
Designed by Sam Whibley

Reading consultants: Alison Kelly and Anne Washtell

First published in 2019 by Usborne Publishing Ltd., Usborne House, 83-85 Saffron Hill, London EC1N 8RT, England.
www.usborne.com Copyright © 2019 Usborne Publishing Ltd.